MARGARET RYAN

Robbie and the Pirate

Illustrated by Bridget MacKeith

MACDONALD YOUNG BOOKS

Robbie liked school. He liked Miss Dobbs his teacher and PE and art. He also liked making rude noises through his straw when he had his lunch-time drink. But he didn't like walking to and from school.
That could be scary.

Scary Thing Number One

Growler lived at number ten.
Every time Robbie passed by the gate,
Growler was there, waiting.
Robbie tried to run past the gate.
Growler growled.

Robbie tried to tiptoe past the gate.
Growler growled.
Robbie tried to whistle, to make
Growler think he wasn't scared.
Growler growled so loudly he set off
all the other dogs in the street.
And Robbie ran, right into –

Scary Thing Number Two

Tiger lived at number forty.
Every time Robbie passed by the gate,
Tiger was there, waiting.
Robbie tried to run past the gate.
Tiger hissed.

8

Robbie tried to tiptoe past the gate.
Tiger hissed.
Robbie tried to whistle, to make
Tiger think he wasn't scared.
Tiger hissed and jumped at Robbie.
And Robbie ran, right into –

Scary Thing Number Three

The Grump twins lived at the end
of the street. Every time Robbie passed
by their gate, they were there, waiting.
Robbie tried to run past the gate.
The Grump twins called him names –
"Smelly Socks" or "Pie Face".

Robbie tried to tiptoe past their gate.
The Grump twins threw mud pies –
"Gotcha, Robbie!" **Splat!**
Robbie tried to whistle to make them
think he wasn't scared. The Grump
twins chased him right round the
corner and into school.

Robbie nearly always felt safe at school, but not today.

Today there was a big black hat hanging on his coat peg. There were big black boots where Robbie kept his wellies. And sitting in Robbie's seat, was a pirate with a big black beard.

"Oh no!" said Robbie.

Robbie took a deep breath. He was just going to ask the pirate to give him back his seat, when Miss Dobbs said, "This is Blackbeard. He's come to school to learn to read and write."

13

"I never had time
to learn before,"
grinned Blackbeard.
"Too busy boiling
people in oil!"

Robbie sat in another seat.

The first lesson that day was maths.

Miss Dobbs asked Blackbeard to give
out the maths books. Blackbeard took
Robbie's maths book and started
writing in it.

Robbie took a deep breath. He was just going to ask Blackbeard to give him back his book, when Miss Dobbs said,

"I'll teach you maths now, Blackbeard."

16

"I never had time to learn before," grinned Blackbeard. "Too busy making people walk the plank."

Robbie got a piece of paper for his maths lesson.

Soon it was lunchtime. Robbie was
in the line behind Blackbeard.
And Blackbeard was hungry.
Very hungry. He had the last two
helpings of sausages and chips.
This left only green beans for Robbie.

Robbie took a deep breath. He was just going to tell Blackbeard that he needed some food too, when the dinner lady said,

"Don't eat with your fingers, Blackbeard, I'll show you how to use a knife and fork."

"I never had time to learn before," grinned Blackbeard. "Too busy fighting nasty pirates."
Robbie ate the green beans.

That afternoon they had art. Robbie
drew a picture of a pirate with a
black beard eating sausages and chips.
He used so much paint the picture
still wasn't dry at home time.

"You'll have to carry it home, Robbie,"
said Miss Dobbs.
Robbie carried it as far as the Grump
twins' gate. The Grump twins were
there, waiting.

23

"What's this?" they cried, grabbing
the painting. "A silly pirate with
a silly black beard!"
"Do you mean me?" asked Blackbeard.
The Grump twins turned round.
"Help!" they said. They dropped the
painting and ran back into their house.

"Nice painting, Robbie," smiled
Blackbeard. "No one's ever done
a painting of me. I never had time
to have a friend before."

Robbie smiled back. "You can keep the painting if you like, for helping me with scary thing number three." Then Robbie told Blackbeard all about the other two scary things. "I'll walk home with you, Robbie," said Blackbeard.

When they reached number forty
Tiger was there, waiting.
Robbie and Blackbeard walked past.
Tiger hissed.
Blackbeard hissed right back.
Tiger ran back into her house.

When they reached number ten
Growler was there, waiting.
Robbie and Blackbeard walked past.
Growler growled.
Blackbeard growled right back.
Growler ran back
into his house.

Robbie grinned at Blackbeard.
"Would you like to come to my house
for tea?" he said. "It's pizza tonight."

"I love pizza," said Blackbeard, "but I'm not very good with a knife and fork yet."

"That's all right," said Robbie.

"It's take-away pizza. We always eat it with our fingers!"